'Twas the Night Before a GREEN Christmas

as told by a real life SNOWMAN

Tracy and Scott Snowman

Real Snowpeople Productions
A Division of Snowman Studios Inc.

There are 39 SNOWPEOPLE inside this book. Some are "real"
and some are illustrated. Can you find them all?
Visit www.realsnowpeople.com to find the locations of all 39
and find out why there are exactly 39.

For Taylor and Jake

'Twas two nights before Christmas when through the North Pole
the wind was not stirring, nor any bright soul.

The fireplace was lit for the evening with care
and Santa's red socks were drying midair.

The Clauses' were snuggled all warm in their bed
when the cracking of ice raised both of their heads.

With mamma in her ear muffs and I in my cap
we had just settled in for a long chilly nap.

When out on the tundra there arose such a clatter,
we sprang from our snowbank to see what was the matter.

Away to Santa's window we rolled like a flash
when we slipped in the snow and made a big splash.

The moon lit the scene of the puddle below.
Santa gasped at the sight of the melting snow.

He called for his reindeer who soon would appear.

They came running and pawing unable to steer.

With Christmas so close and footing so slick
we knew in a moment we had to think quick.

With breath full of magic and a whistle so sweet
we blew up a wind at the reindeers' feet.

Now, Dasher! Now, Dancer! Now, Prancer and Vixen!
On, Comet! On, Cupid! On, Donner and Blitzen!

To the top of the trees now make your big funnel.
Spiral up, spin fast and make a wind tunnel.

As the kiss of cool wind turned the puddles to snow,
Santa's view out the window returned to it's glow.

So back toward the house we called up to the top
explaining to Santa this warming must STOP.

And then, in a twinkling, it was soon Christmas Eve
a night filled with excitement for those who believe.

As we lifted our heads and were turning around,
Santa leaped to his sleigh without making a sound.

He was dressed all in green from his head to his toes
and he loaded the sleigh with a touch of his nose.

A bag full of toys he had flung in the back
but this year he had something new in the sack.
His plans were now different than ever before
to make the world greener like the suit he now wore.

A green world is cooler, he thought and he mused.
We all must recycle, reduce and reuse.
As he made his first landing and slid down the flue,
he refilled the stockings with toys old and new.

The old toys were special and rebuilt by hand
so no toy was wasted and put in the land.

to Stay on "NICE" LIST.

- Turn OFF lights when leaving a room.
- Turn OFF electric items such as computers, printers, and TV's when not in use.
- Switch to fluorescent light bulbs since 8-10 years and use less energy.
- Use washing machines and dishes when there is a completely full.
- Turn your heater down by a few air-conditioner up a few
- Take shorter showers
- Recycle paper, glass so much to save water
- Share car rides transportation
- Drive slower (this saves
- Ride a b
- Wash

The cookies came next. The milk went down fast.
He left them a list to make the world last.

His quick, nimble fingers went straight back to work.
He screwed in new light bulbs and turned with a jerk.

With a stroke of his beard
and a wink of his eye,
he made the cans for recycling fly right by.

He knew with some help he could make a big dent.
His friends would be happy the message was sent.

The Earth is worth saving one step at a time
and much of the effort does not cost a dime.

We heard him exclaim as he drove out of sight,
"Merry Christmas to all and to all a green night!"

How to Stay on Santa's "NICE" LIST:

- Turn OFF lights when leaving a room.
- Turn OFF electric items such as computers, printers, and TV's when not in use.
- Switch to fluorescent light bulbs since they last 8-10 years and use less energy.
- Use washing machines and dishwashers ONLY when there is a completely full load.
- Turn your heater down by a few degrees or your air-conditioner up a few degrees to save energy.
- Take shorter showers or don't fill the bathtub so much to save water.
- Recycle paper, glass, plastic and aluminum cans.
- Share car rides with friends or use public transportation to cut down on gasoline.
- Drive slower when traveling in your car.
- Ride a bicycle or walk when possible.
- Wash the laundry in cold water.
- Plant a tree.

These things will not only help keep our planet cooler and cleaner, but will save your family money too!

For more information, visit our website:
www.realsnowpeople.com

CPSIA information can be obtained
at www.ICGtesting.com
Printed in the USA
259401LV00008BA

9 780983 424406